IRRADIATED BY COSMIC RAYS AND TRANSFORMED TO POSSESS SUPERHUMAN POWERS, THEY JOINED TOGETHER TO FIGHT EVIL. **MISTER FANTASTIC,** THE **INVISIBLE WOMAN,** THE **HUMAN TORCH** AND THE **THING.** TOGETHER THEY CALL THEMSELVES THE FANTASTIC FOUR

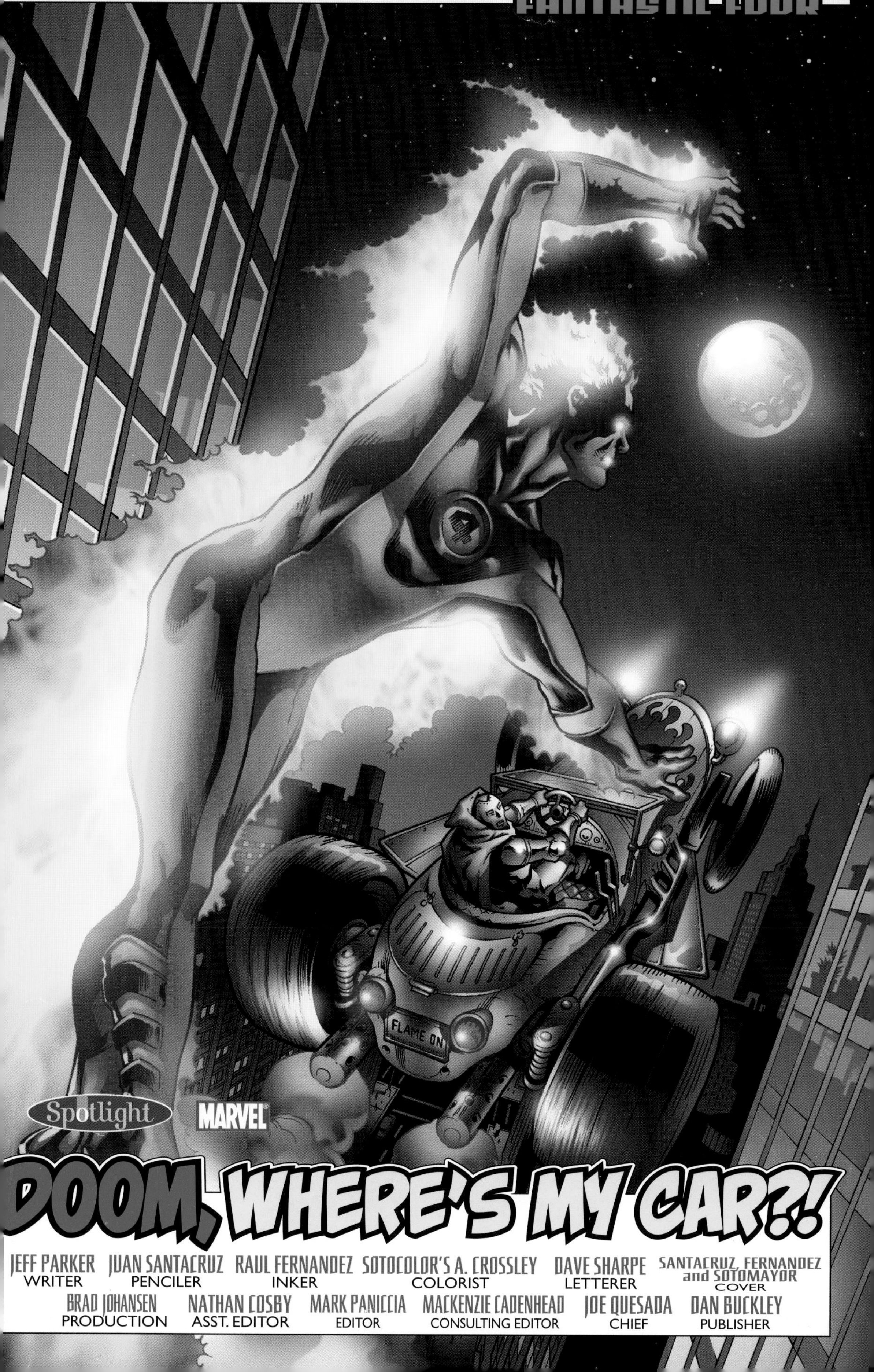
FLAME ON

Spotlight MARVEL

DOOM, WHERE'S MY CAR?!

JEFF PARKER WRITER · JUAN SANTACRUZ PENCILER · RAUL FERNANDEZ INKER · SOTOCOLOR'S A. CROSSLEY COLORIST · DAVE SHARPE LETTERER · SANTACRUZ, FERNANDEZ and SOTOMAYOR COVER

BRAD JOHANSEN PRODUCTION · NATHAN COSBY ASST. EDITOR · MARK PANICCIA EDITOR · MACKENZIE CADENHEAD CONSULTING EDITOR · JOE QUESADA CHIEF · DAN BUCKLEY PUBLISHER

VISIT US AT
www.abdopublishing.com

Reinforced library bound edition published in 2008 by Spotlight, a division of the ABDO Publishing Group, 8000 West 78th Street, Edina, Minnesota 55439. Spotlight produces high-quality reinforced library bound editions for schools and libraries. Published by agreement with Marvel Characters, Inc.

Library of Congress Cataloging-in-Publication Data

Parker, Jeff, 1966-
  Doom, where's my car?! / Jeff Parker, writer ; Juan Santacruz, penciler ; Raul Fernandez, inker ; A. Crossley, colorist ; Dave Sharpe, letterer ; Santacruz, Fernandez and Sotomayor, cover. -- Reinforced library bound ed.
      p. cm. -- (Fantastic Four)
  "Marvel age"--Cover.
  Revision of issue 12 of Marvel adventures Fantastic Four.
  ISBN 978-1-59961-389-5
  1. Graphic novels. I. Santacruz, Juan. II. Marvel adventures Fantastic Four. 12. III. Title.

PN6728.F33P35 2008
741.5'973--dc22

                                                      2007020247

All Spotlight books have reinforced library bindings and
are manufactured in the United States of America.

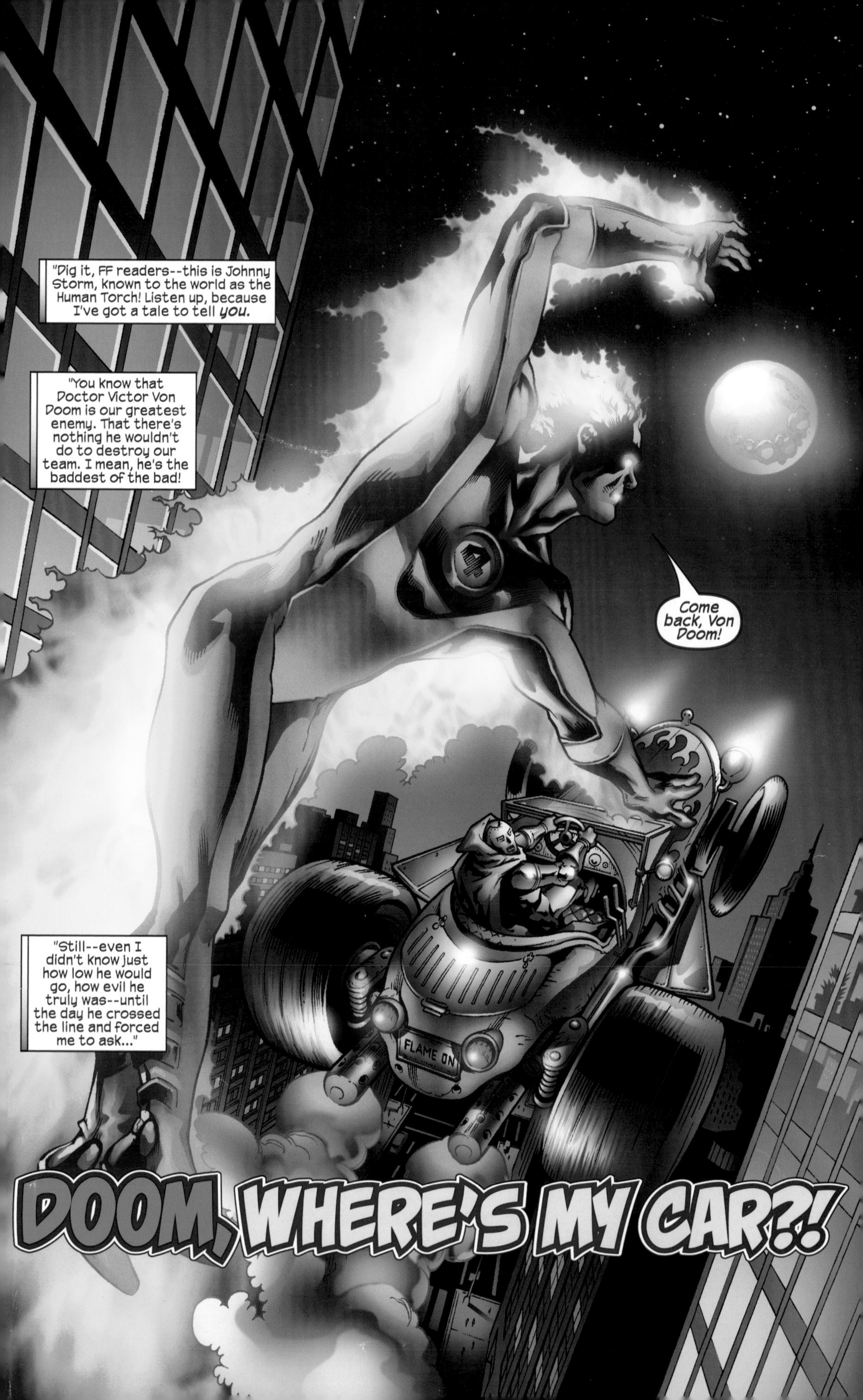
"Dig it, FF readers--this is Johnny Storm, known to the world as the Human Torch! Listen up, because I've got a tale to tell *you*.
"You know that Doctor Victor Von Doom is our greatest enemy. That there's nothing he wouldn't do to destroy our team. I mean, he's the baddest of the bad!
Come back, Von Doom!
"Still--even I didn't know just how low he would go, how evil he truly was--until the day he crossed the line and forced me to ask..."
FLAME ON
DOOM, WHERE'S MY CAR?!

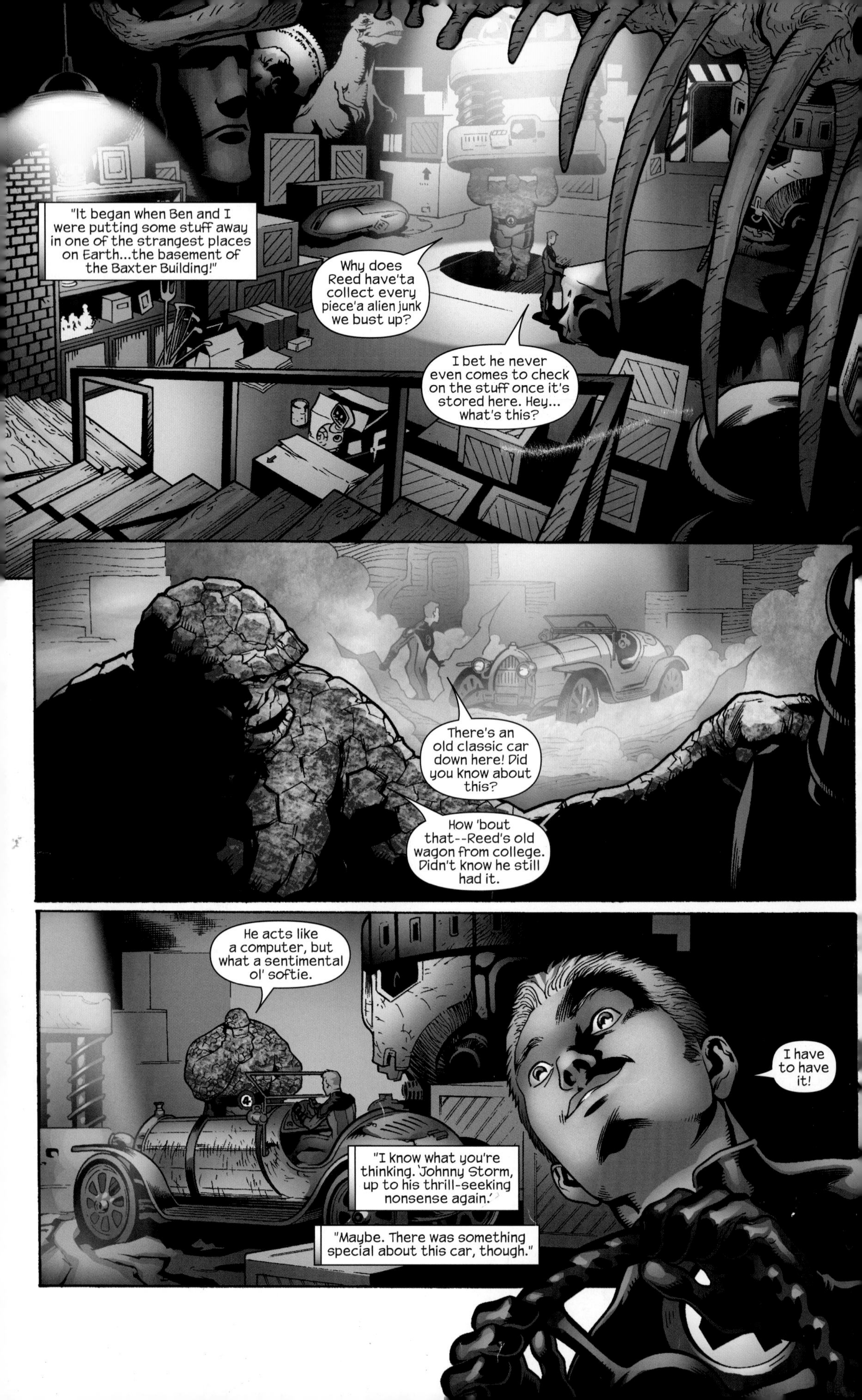
"It began when Ben and I were putting some stuff away in one of the strangest places on Earth...the basement of the Baxter Building!"
Why does Reed have'ta collect every piece'a alien junk we bust up?
I bet he never even comes to check on the stuff once it's stored here. Hey... what's this?
There's an old classic car down here! Did you know about this?
How 'bout that--Reed's old wagon from college. Didn't know he still had it.
He acts like a computer, but what a sentimental ol' softie.
I have to have it!
"I know what you're thinking. 'Johnny Storm, up to his thrill-seeking nonsense again.'
"Maybe. There was something special about this car, though."

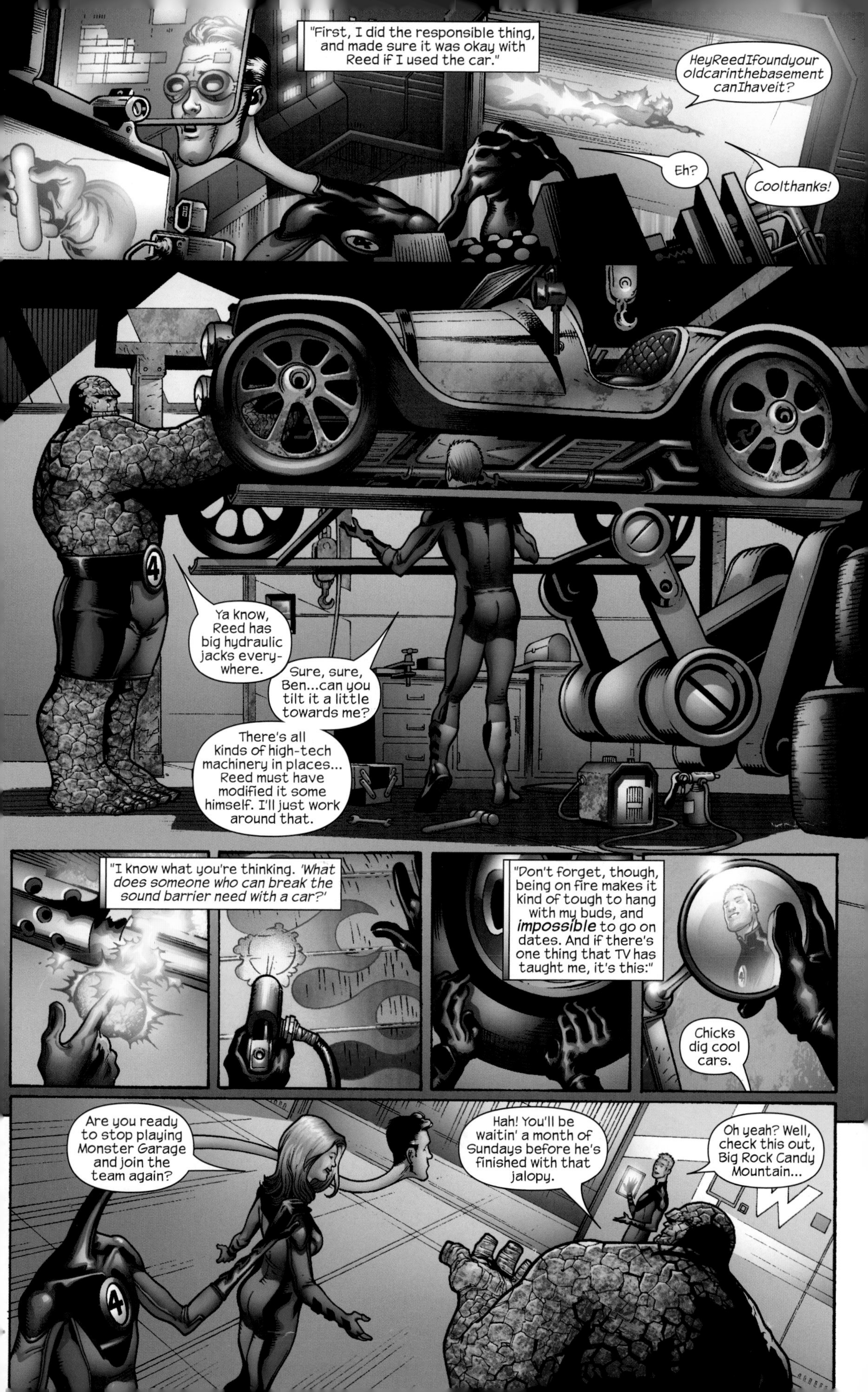
"First, I did the responsible thing, and made sure it was okay with Reed if I used the car."
HeyReedIfoundyour oldcarinthebasement canIhaveit?
Eh?
Coolthanks!
Ya know, Reed has big hydraulic jacks every-where.
Sure, sure, Ben...can you tilt it a little towards me?
There's all kinds of high-tech machinery in places... Reed must have modified it some himself. I'll just work around that.
"I know what you're thinking. 'What does someone who can break the sound barrier need with a car?'
"Don't forget, though, being on fire makes it kind of tough to hang with my buds, and impossible to go on dates. And if there's one thing that TV has taught me, it's this:"
Chicks dig cool cars.
Are you ready to stop playing Monster Garage and join the team again?
Hah! You'll be waitin' a month of Sundays before he's finished with that jalopy.
Oh yeah? Well, check this out, Big Rock Candy Mountain...

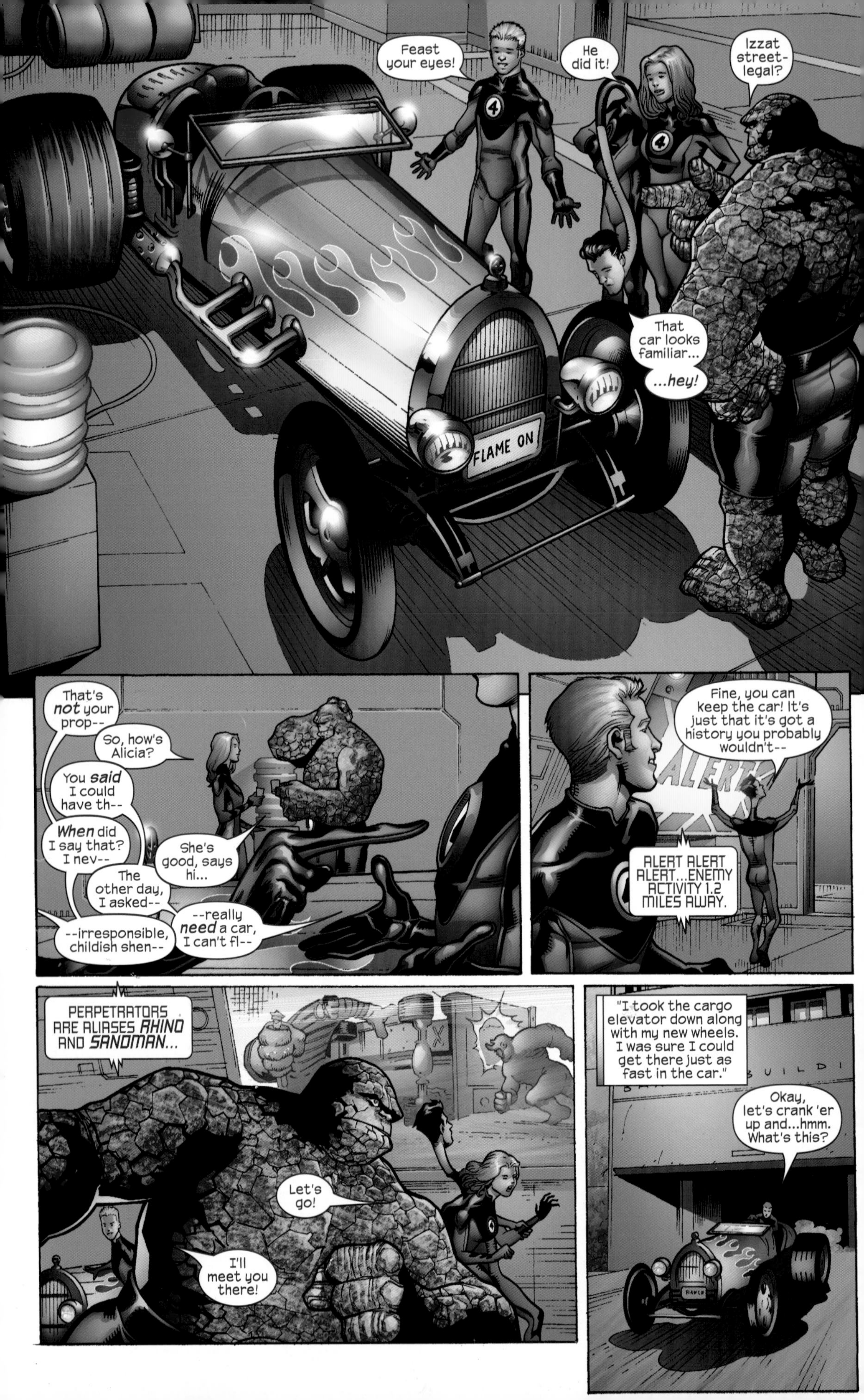
Feast your eyes!
He did it!
Izzat street-legal?
That car looks familiar...
...hey!
FLAME ON
That's not your prop--
So, how's Alicia?
You said I could have th--
When did I say that? I nev--
She's good, says hi...
The other day, I asked--
--really need a car, I can't fl--
--irresponsible, childish shen--
Fine, you can keep the car! It's just that it's got a history you probably wouldn't--
ALERT ALERT ALERT...ENEMY ACTIVITY 1.2 MILES AWAY.
PERPETRATORS ARE ALIASES RHINO AND SANDMAN...
Let's go!
I'll meet you there!
"I took the cargo elevator down along with my new wheels. I was sure I could get there just as fast in the car."
Okay, let's crank 'er up and...hmm. What's this?

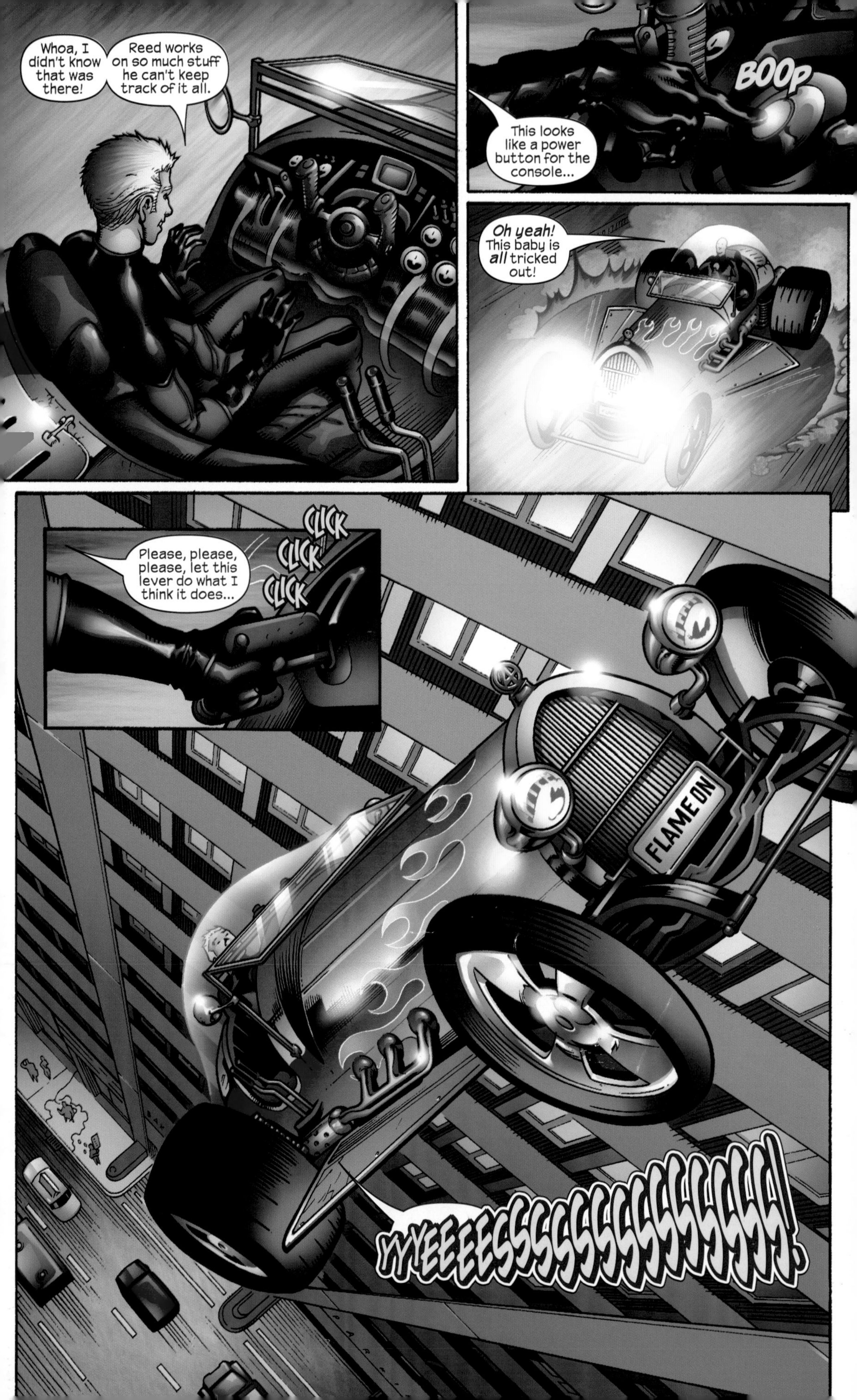

Whoa, I didn't know that was there!
Reed works on so much stuff he can't keep track of it all.
BOOP
This looks like a power button for the console...
Oh yeah! This baby is ***all*** tricked out!
CLICK
CLICK
CLICK
Please, please, please, let this lever do what I think it does...
FLAME ON
YYYEEEESSSSSSSSSSSSSS!

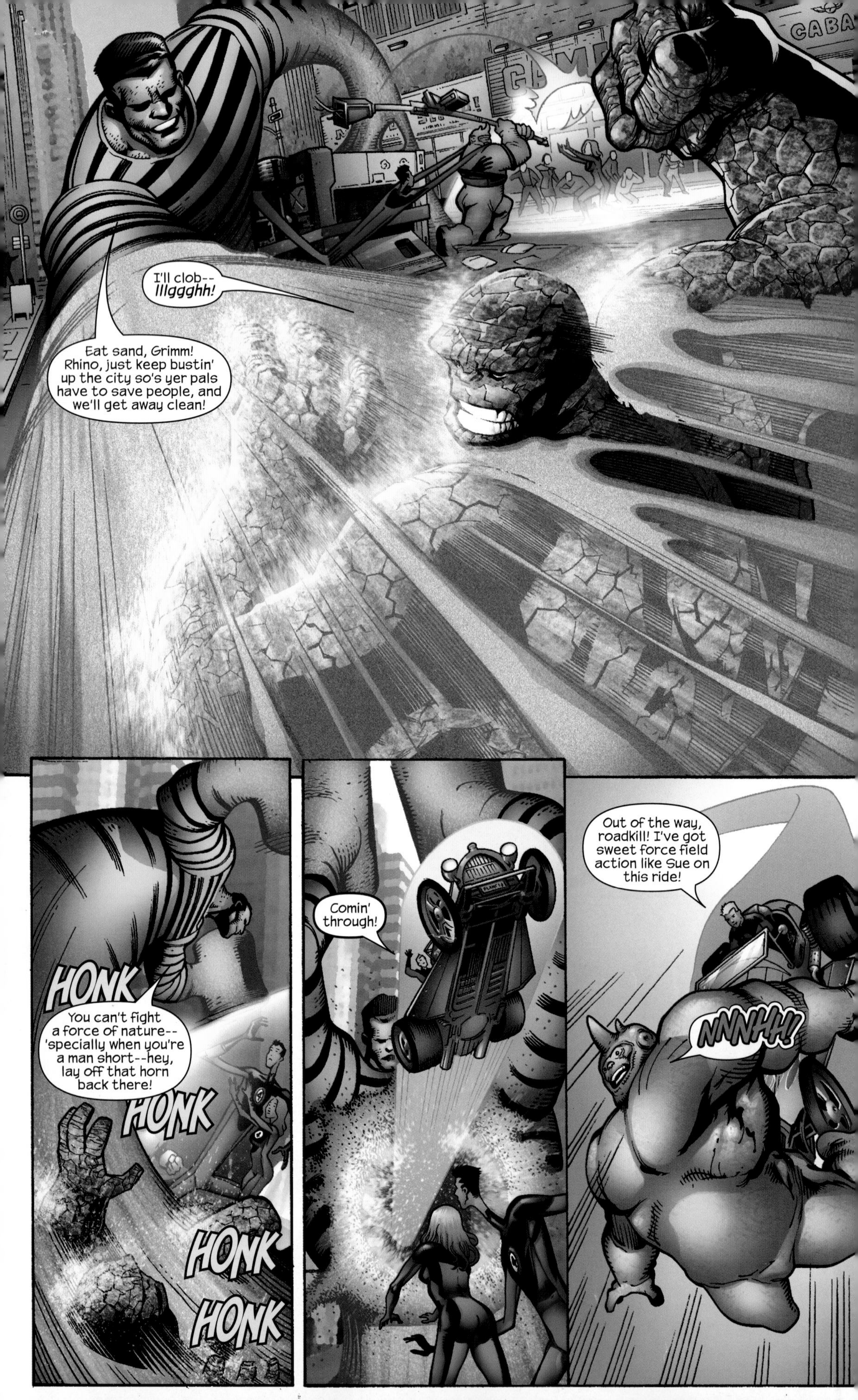
I'll clob--
lllggghh!
Eat sand, Grimm! Rhino, just keep bustin' up the city so's yer pals have to save people, and we'll get away clean!
HONK
You can't fight a force of nature--'specially when you're a man short--hey, lay off that horn back there!
HONK
HONK
HONK
Comin' through!
Out of the way, roadkill! I've got sweet force field action like Sue on this ride!
NNNHH!

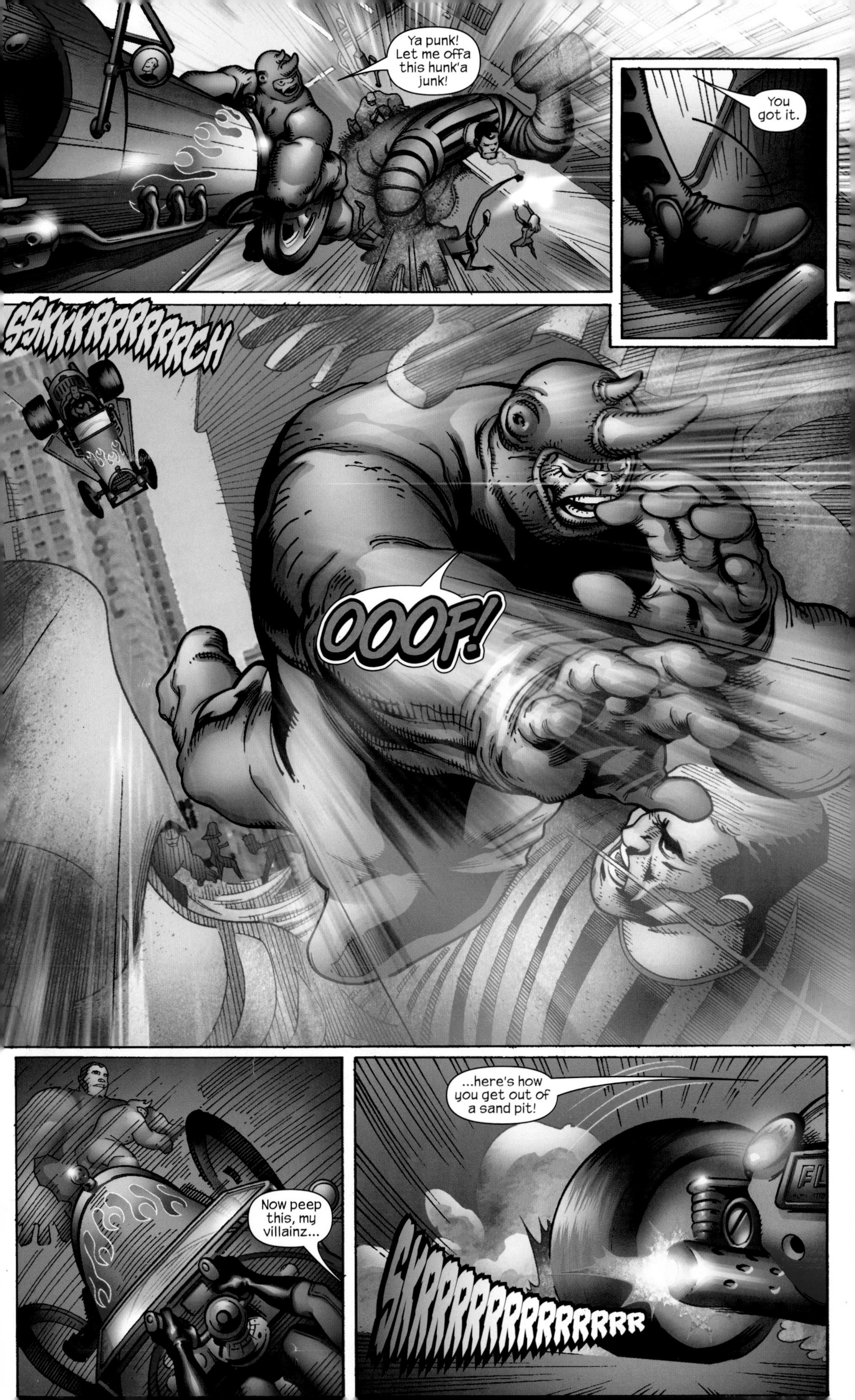
Ya punk! Let me offa this hunk'a junk!
You got it.
SSKKKRRRRRRCH
OOOF!
Now peep this, my villainz...
...here's how you get out of a sand pit!
SKRRRRRRRRRRRRR

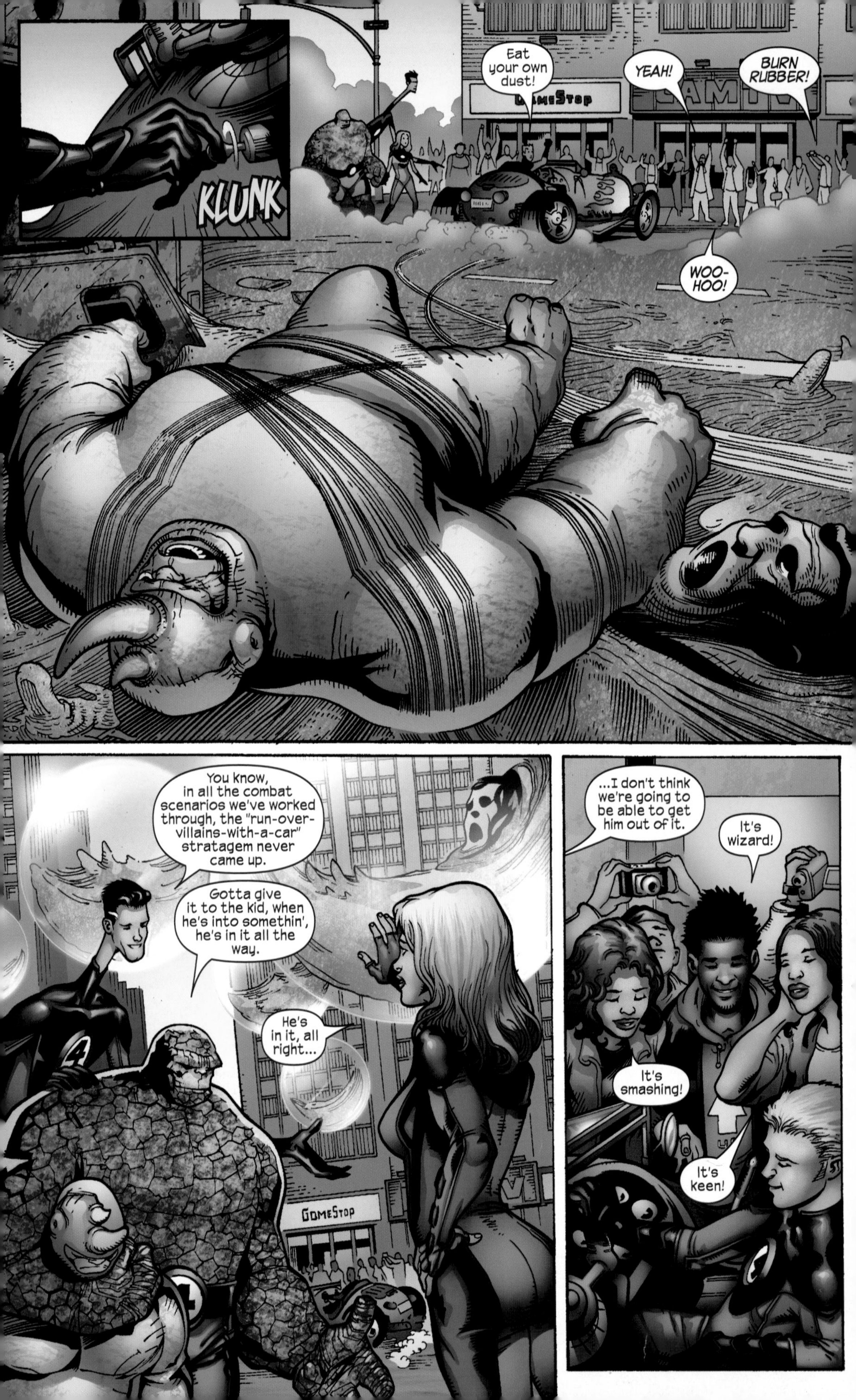
KLUNK
Eat your own dust!
YEAH!
BURN RUBBER!
WOO-HOO!
You know, in all the combat scenarios we've worked through, the "run-over-villains-with-a-car" stratagem never came up.
Gotta give it to the kid, when he's into somethin', he's in it all the way.
He's in it, all right...
...I don't think we're going to be able to get him out of it.
It's wizard!
It's smashing!
It's keen!

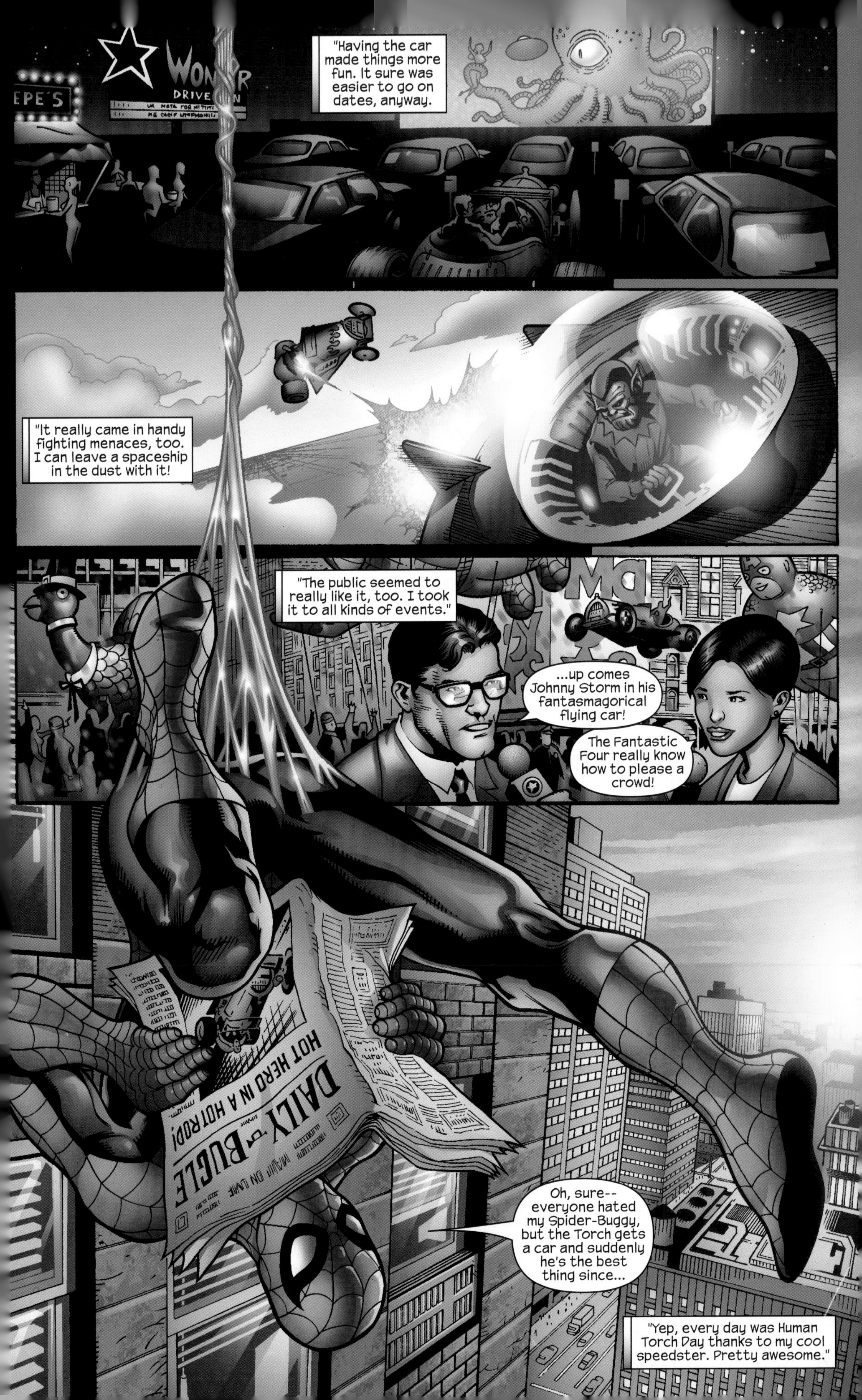
"Having the car made things more fun. It sure was easier to go on dates, anyway.
"It really came in handy fighting menaces, too. I can leave a spaceship in the dust with it!
"The public seemed to really like it, too. I took it to all kinds of events."
...up comes Johnny Storm in his fantasmagorical flying car!
The Fantastic Four really know how to please a crowd!
DAILY BUGLE
HOT HERO IN A HOT ROD!
Oh, sure-- everyone hated my Spider-Buggy, but the Torch gets a car and suddenly he's the best thing since...
"Yep, every day was Human Torch Day thanks to my cool speedster. Pretty awesome."

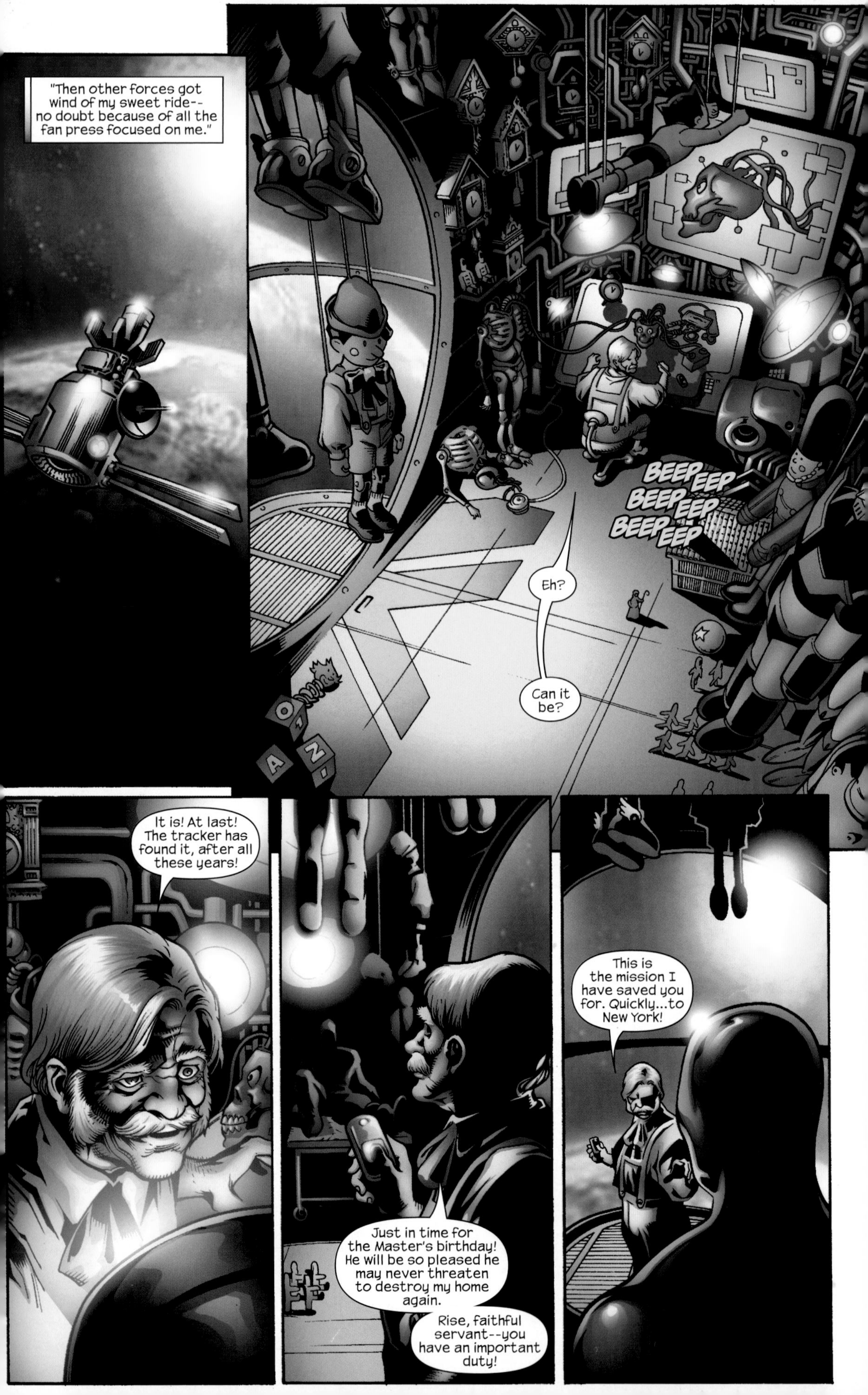
"Then other forces got wind of my sweet ride--no doubt because of all the fan press focused on me."
BEEPEEP BEEPEEP BEEPEEP
Eh?
Can it be?
It is! At last! The tracker has found it, after all these years!
Just in time for the Master's birthday! He will be so pleased he may never threaten to destroy my home again.
Rise, faithful servant--you have an important duty!
This is the mission I have saved you for. Quickly...to New York!

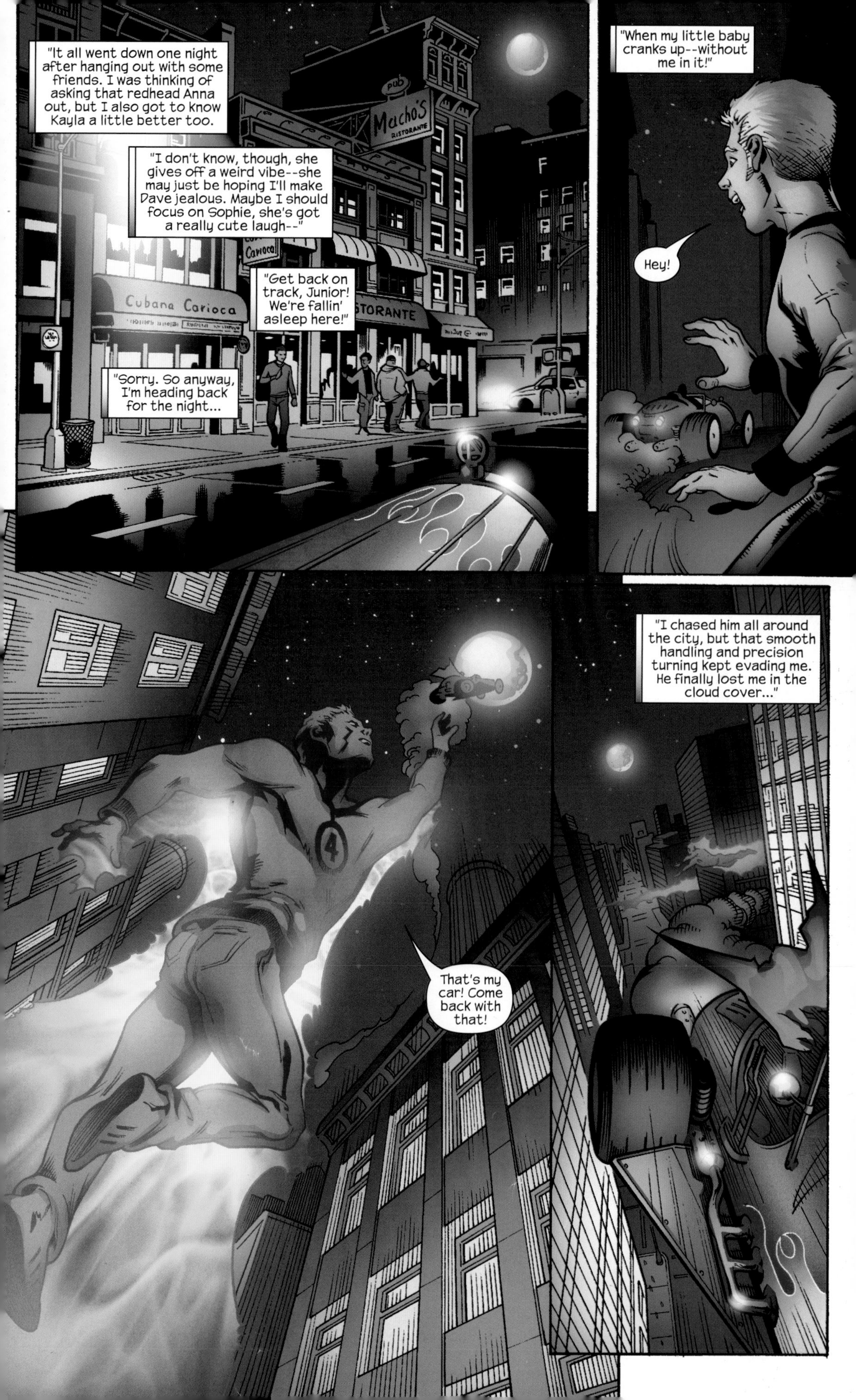
"It all went down one night after hanging out with some friends. I was thinking of asking that redhead Anna out, but I also got to know Kayla a little better too.
"I don't know, though, she gives off a weird vibe--she may just be hoping I'll make Dave jealous. Maybe I should focus on Sophie, she's got a really cute laugh--"
"Get back on track, Junior! We're fallin' asleep here!"
"Sorry. So anyway, I'm heading back for the night...
"When my little baby cranks up--without me in it!"
Hey!
That's my car! Come back with that!
"I chased him all around the city, but that smooth handling and precision turning kept evading me. He finally lost me in the cloud cover..."
Macho's
Ristorante
Pub
Cubana Carioca
Carioca!
STORANTE

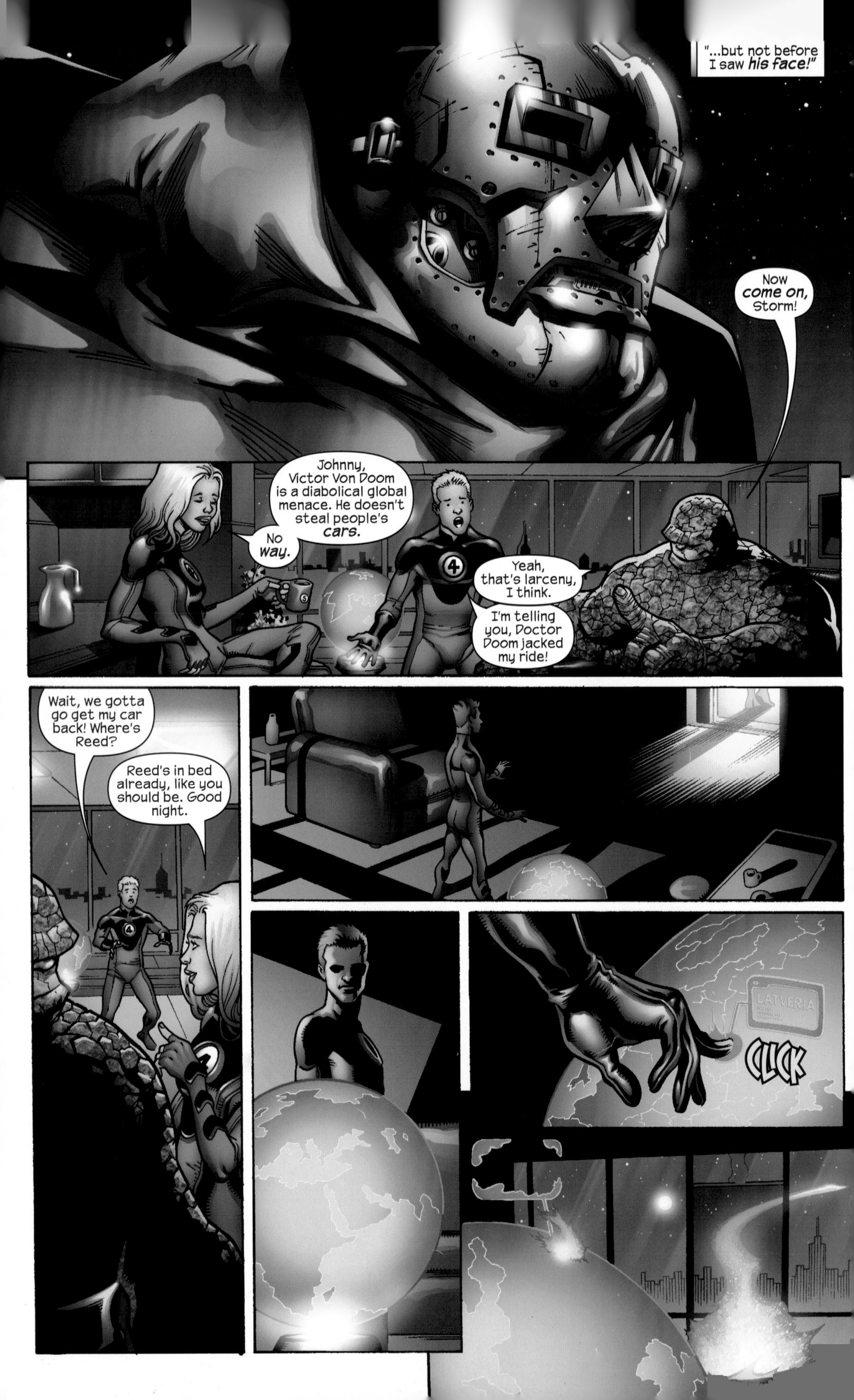
"...but not before I saw his face!"
Now come on, Storm!
No way.
Johnny, Victor Von Doom is a diabolical global menace. He doesn't steal people's cars.
Yeah, that's larceny, I think.
I'm telling you, Doctor Doom jacked my ride!
Wait, we gotta go get my car back! Where's Reed?
Reed's in bed already, like you should be. Good night.
LATVERIA
CLICK

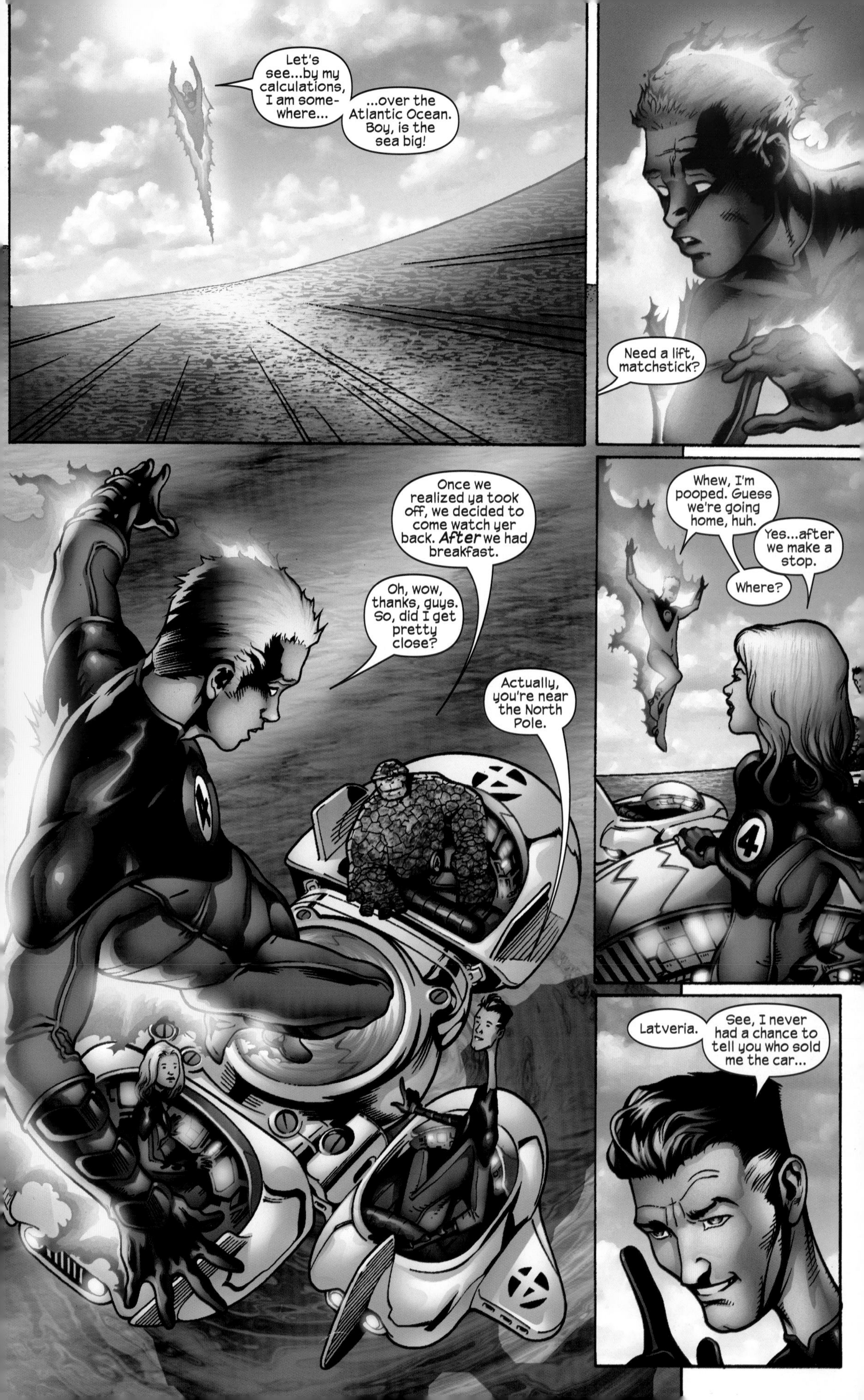
Let's see...by my calculations, I am some-where...
...over the Atlantic Ocean. Boy, is the sea big!
Need a lift, matchstick?
Once we realized ya took off, we decided to come watch yer back. *After* we had breakfast.
Oh, wow, thanks, guys. So, did I get pretty close?
Actually, you're near the North Pole.
Whew, I'm pooped. Guess we're going home, huh.
Yes...after we make a stop.
Where?
Latveria.
See, I never had a chance to tell you who sold me the car...

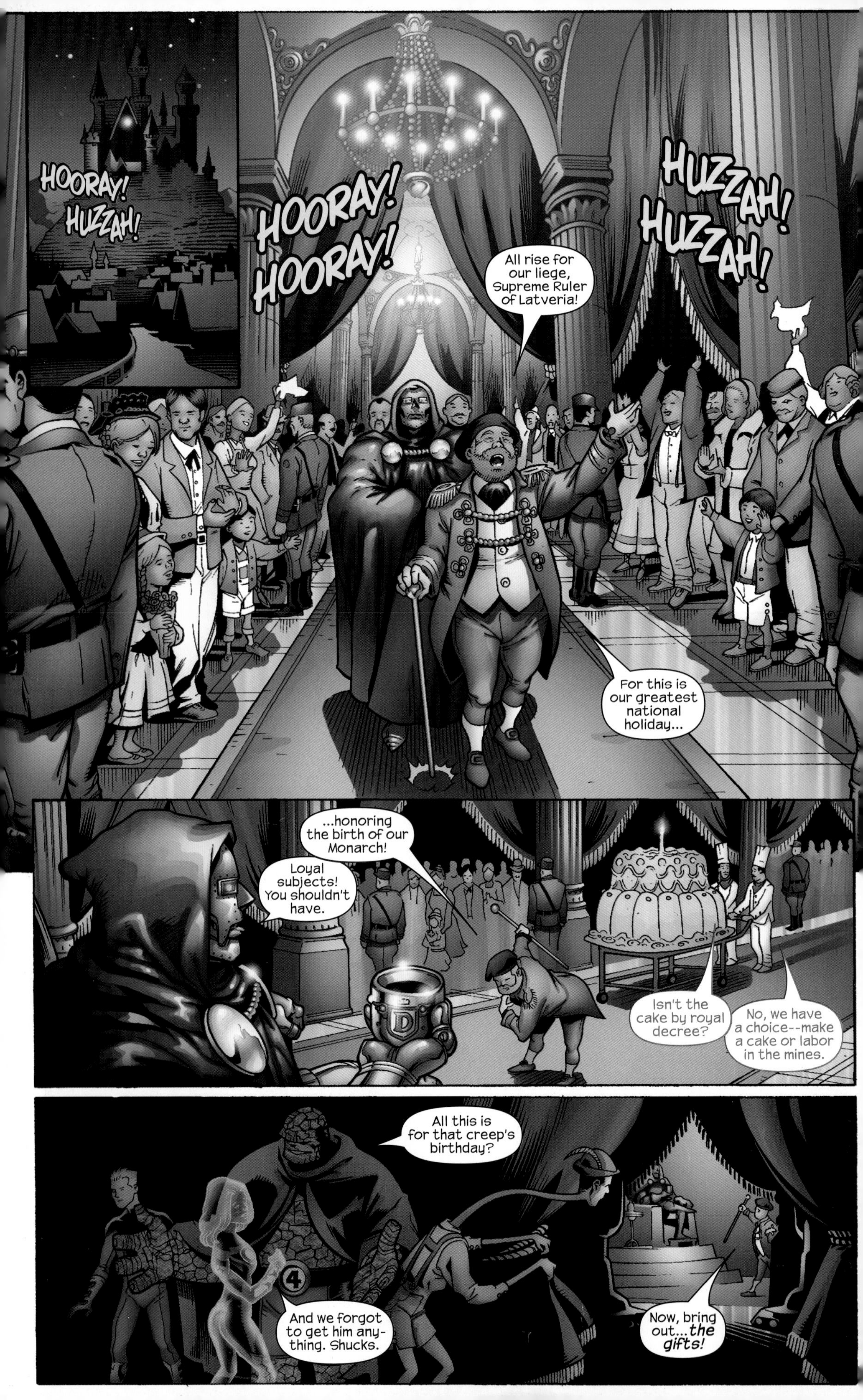
HOORAY! HUZZAH!
HOORAY! HOORAY!
All rise for our liege, Supreme Ruler of Latveria!
HUZZAH! HUZZAH!
For this is our greatest national holiday...
...honoring the birth of our Monarch!
Loyal subjects! You shouldn't have.
Isn't the cake by royal decree?
No, we have a choice--make a cake or labor in the mines.
All this is for that creep's birthday?
And we forgot to get him any-thing. Shucks.
Now, bring out...*the gifts!*

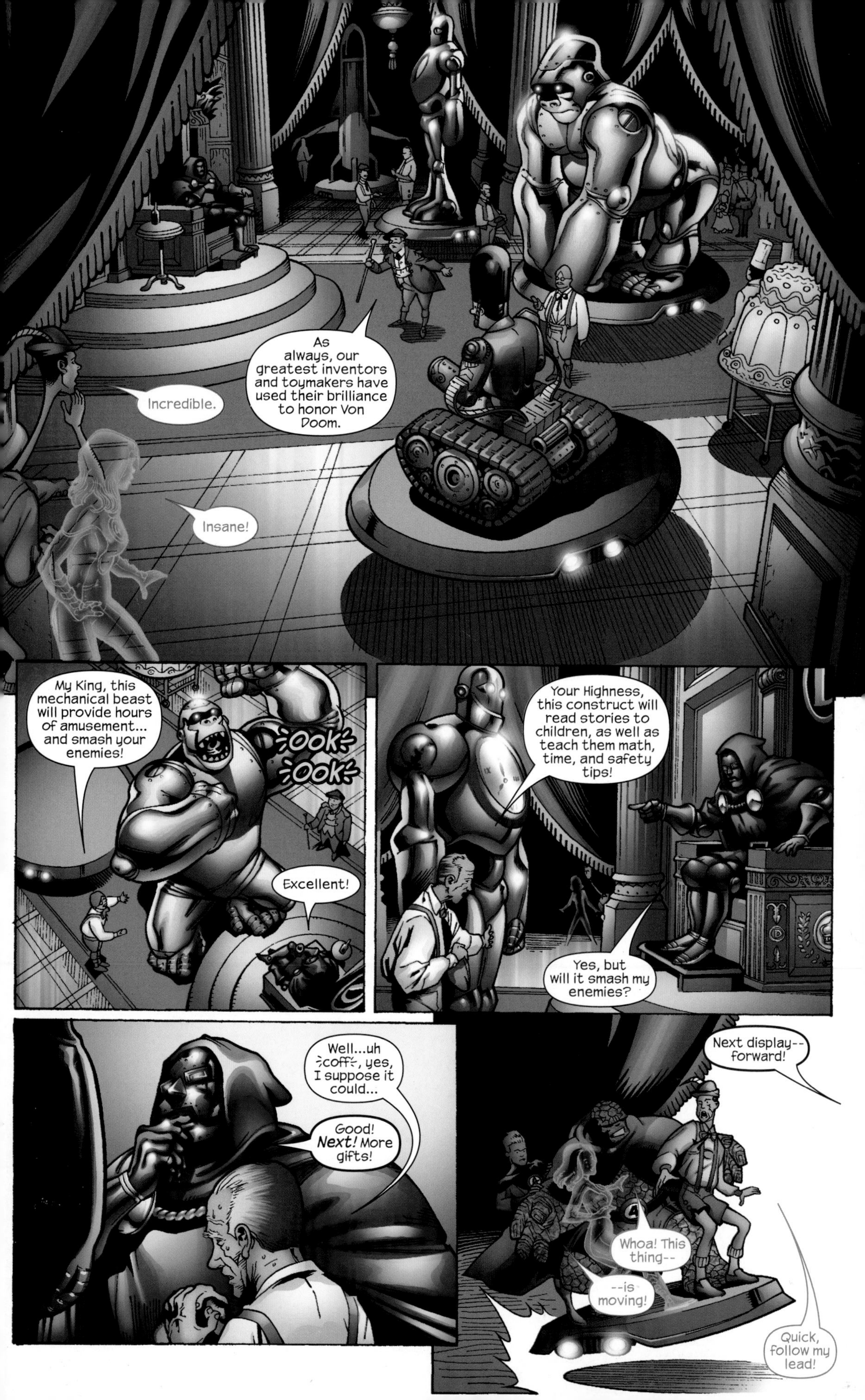
Incredible.
As always, our greatest inventors and toymakers have used their brilliance to honor Von Doom.
Insane!
My King, this mechanical beast will provide hours of amusement... and smash your enemies!
OOK OOK
Excellent!
Your Highness, this construct will read stories to children, as well as teach them math, time, and safety tips!
Yes, but will it smash my enemies?
Well...uh *coff*, yes, I suppose it could...
Good! Next! More gifts!
Next display-- forward!
Whoa! This thing--
--is moving!
Quick, follow my lead!

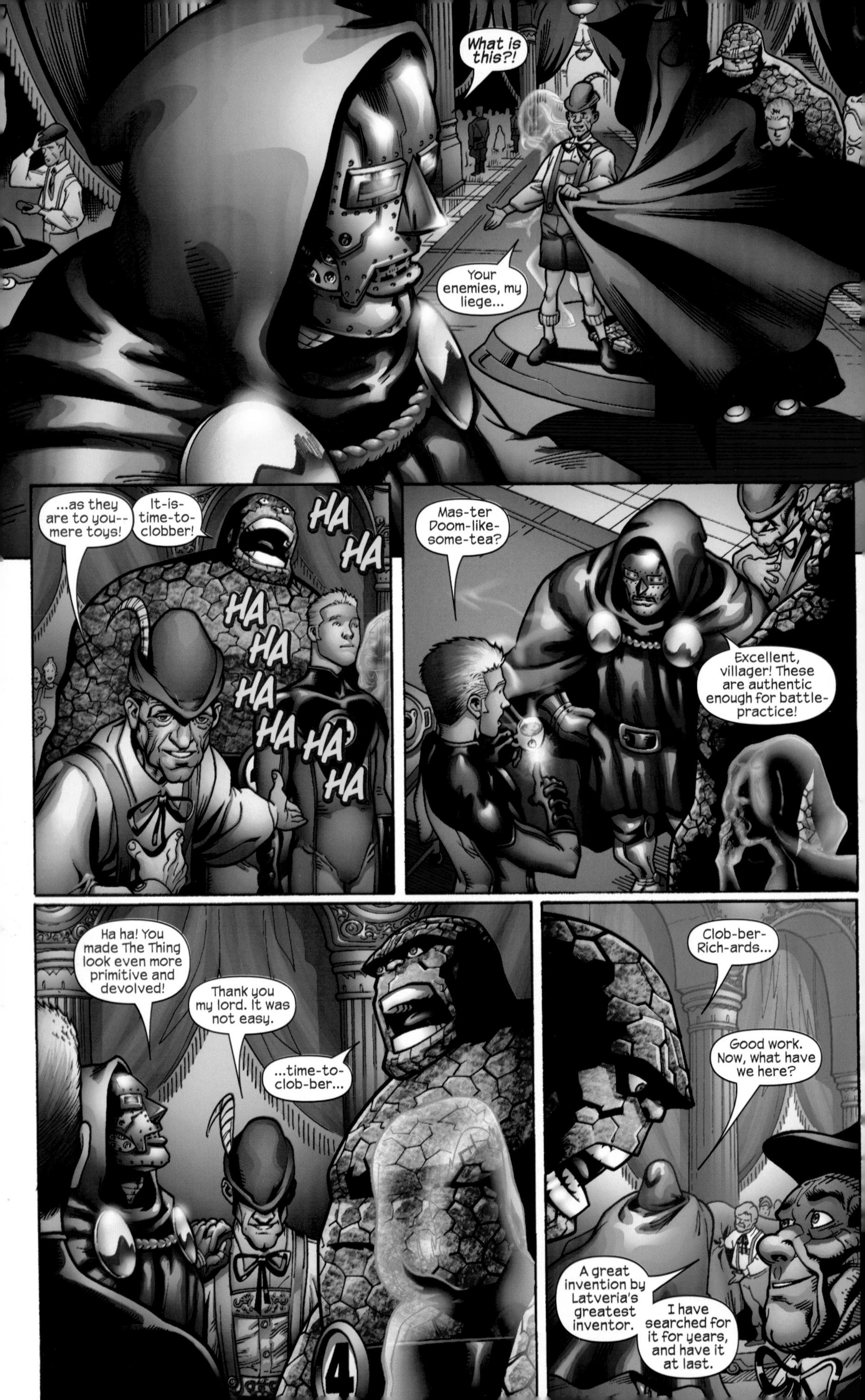
What is this?!
Your enemies, my liege...
...as they are to you-- mere toys!
It-is-time-to-clobber!
HA HA HA HA HA HA HA HA HA
Mas-ter Doom-like-some-tea?
Excellent, villager! These are authentic enough for battle-practice!
Ha ha! You made The Thing look even more primitive and devolved!
Thank you my lord. It was not easy.
...time-to-clob-ber...
Clob-ber-Rich-ards...
Good work. Now, what have we here?
A great invention by Latveria's greatest inventor.
I have searched for it for years, and have it at last.

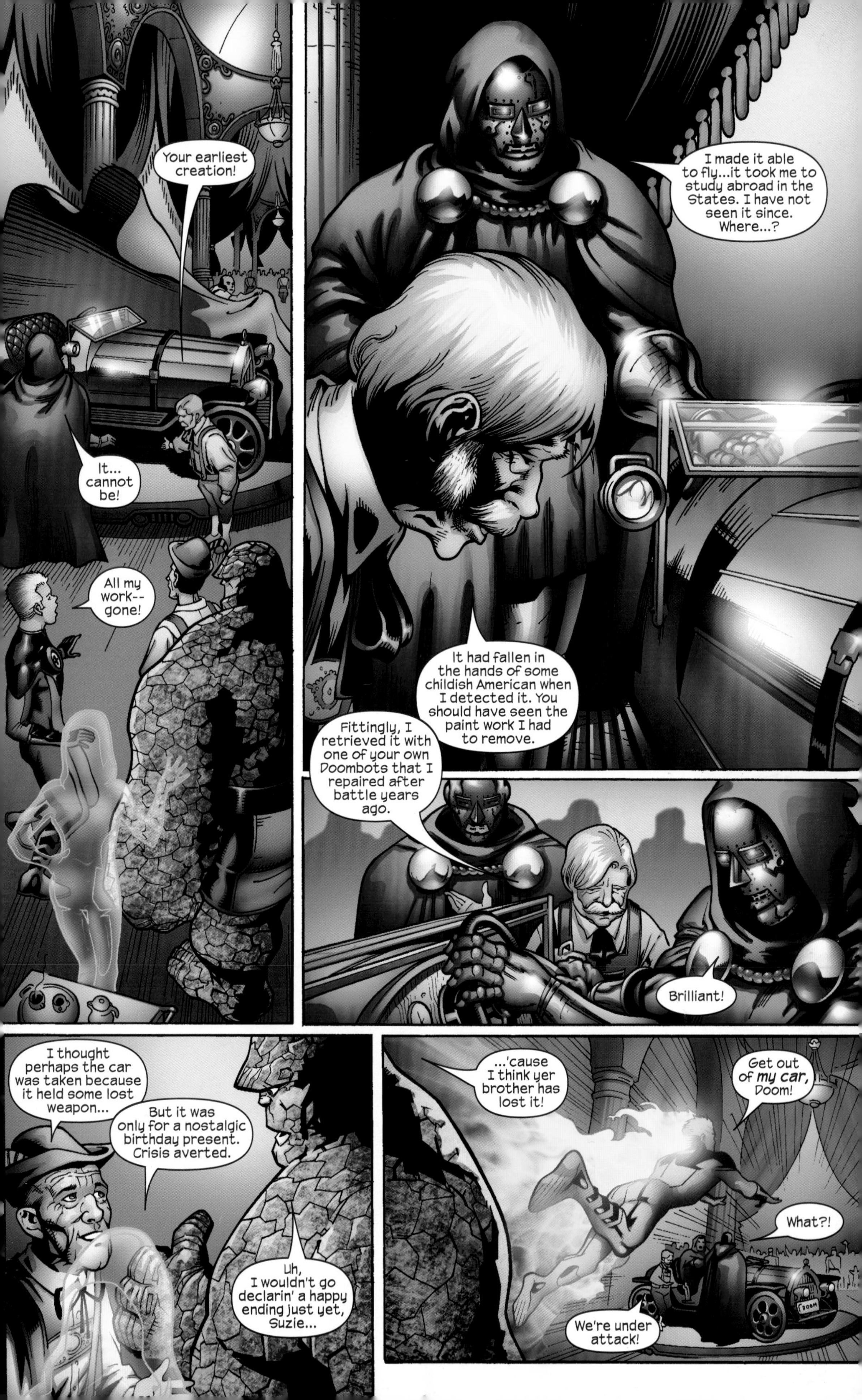
Your earliest creation!
It... cannot be!
All my work-- gone!
I made it able to fly...it took me to study abroad in the States. I have not seen it since. Where...?
It had fallen in the hands of some childish American when I detected it. You should have seen the paint work I had to remove.
Fittingly, I retrieved it with one of your own Doombots that I repaired after battle years ago.
Brilliant!
I thought perhaps the car was taken because it held some lost weapon...
But it was only for a nostalgic birthday present. Crisis averted.
Uh, I wouldn't go declarin' a happy ending just yet, Suzie...
...'cause I think yer brother has lost it!
Get out of my car, Doom!
What?!
We're under attack!
DOOM

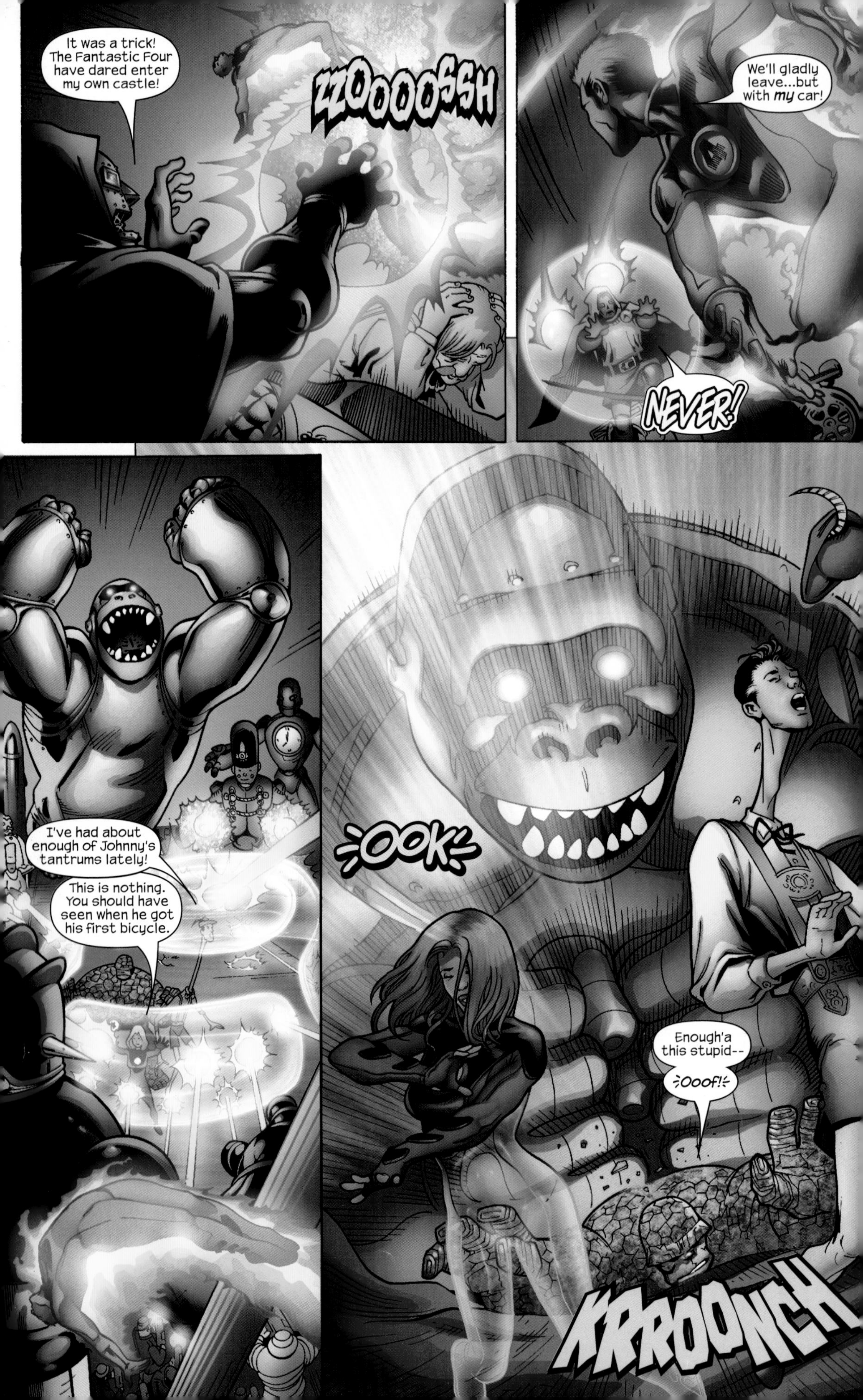
It was a trick! The Fantastic Four have dared enter my own castle!
ZZOOOOOSSH
We'll gladly leave...but with *my* car!
NEVER!
I've had about enough of Johnny's tantrums lately!
This is nothing. You should have seen when he got his first bicycle.
OOK
Enough'a this stupid--
Ooof!
KRROONCH

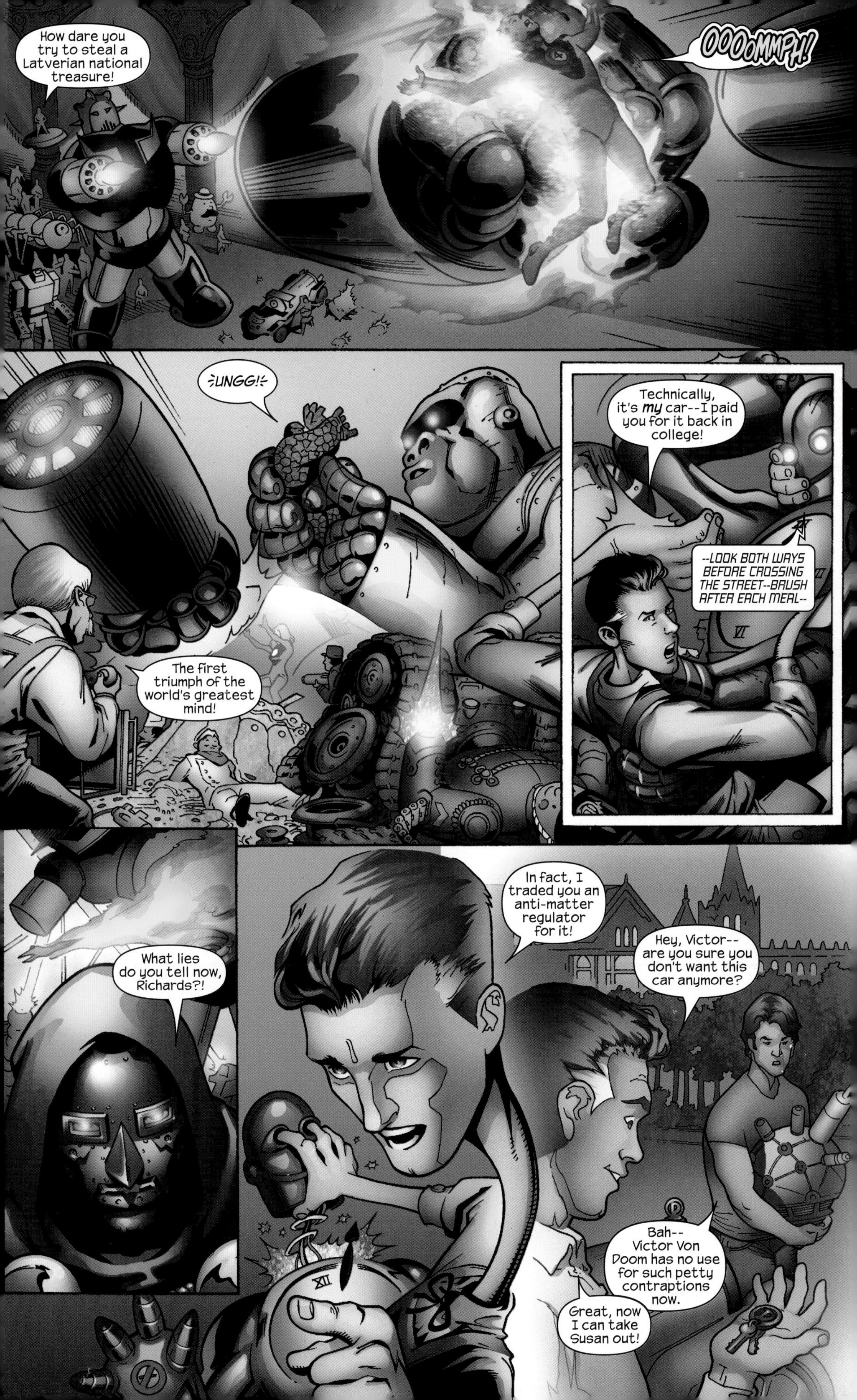
How dare you try to steal a Latverian national treasure!
OOOoMMPH!
UNGG!
The first triumph of the world's greatest mind!
Technically, it's my car--I paid you for it back in college!
--LOOK BOTH WAYS BEFORE CROSSING THE STREET--BRUSH AFTER EACH MEAL--
What lies do you tell now, Richards?!
In fact, I traded you an anti-matter regulator for it!
Hey, Victor--are you sure you don't want this car anymore?
Bah--Victor Von Doom has no use for such petty contraptions now.
Great, now I can take Susan out!

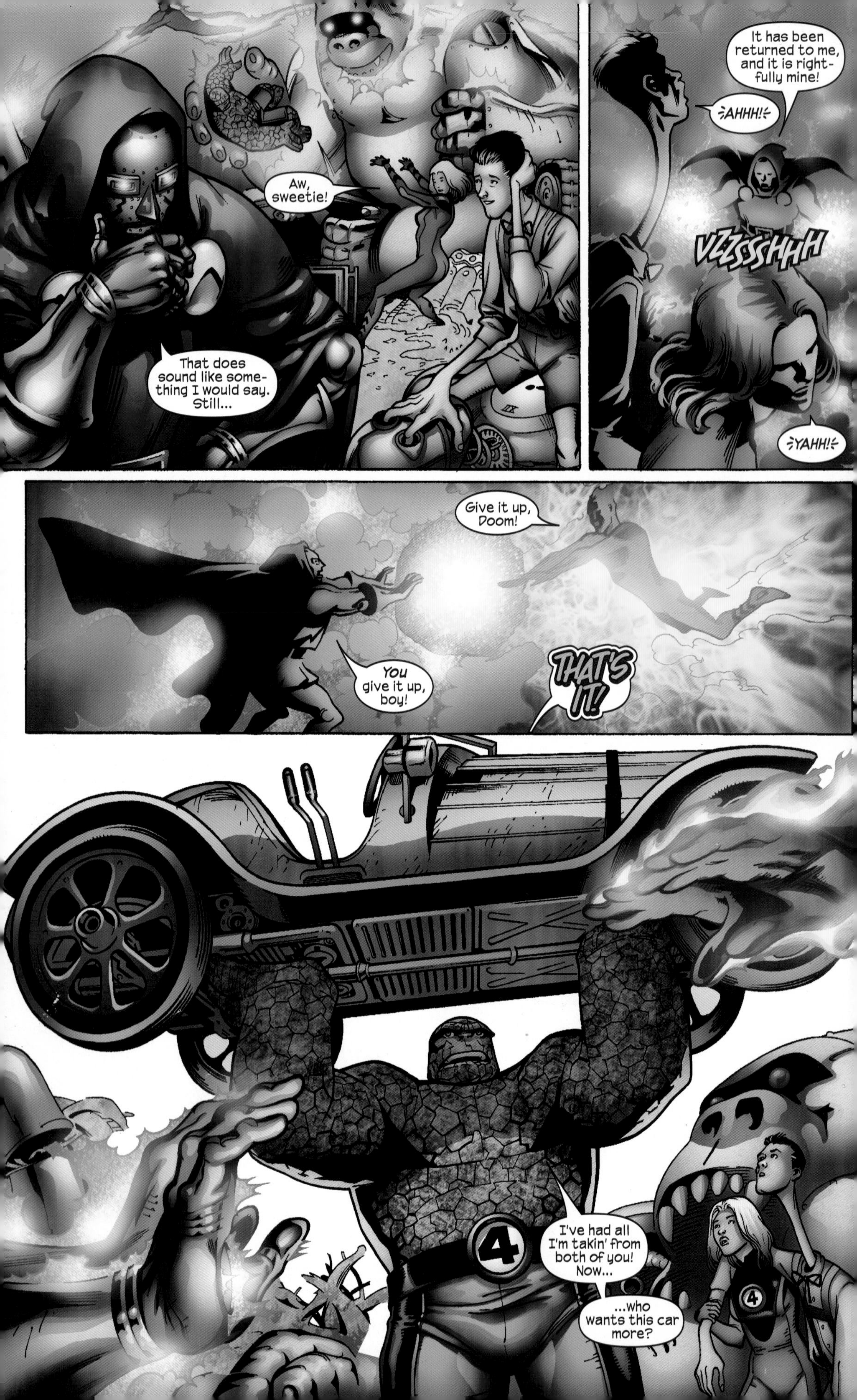
Aw, sweetie!
That does sound like some-thing I would say. Still...
It has been returned to me, and it is right-fully mine!
AHHH!
VZZSSHHH
YAHH!
Give it up, Doom!
You give it up, boy!
THAT'S IT!
I've had all I'm takin' from both of you! Now...
...who wants this car more?

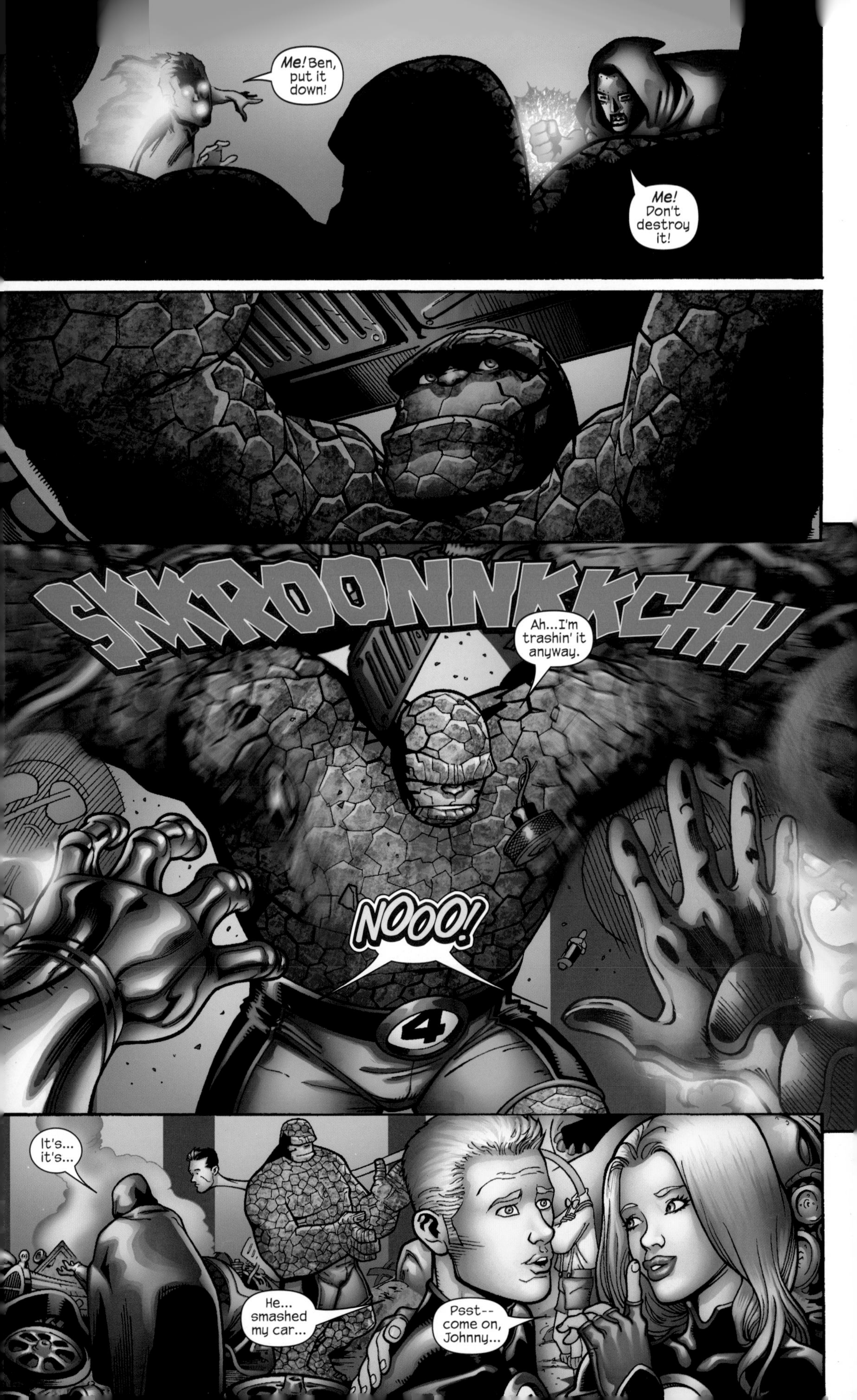
Me! Ben, put it down!
Me! Don't destroy it!
SKKROONNKKCHH
Ah...I'm trashin' it anyway.
NOOO!
It's... it's...
He... smashed my car...
Psst-- come on, Johnny...

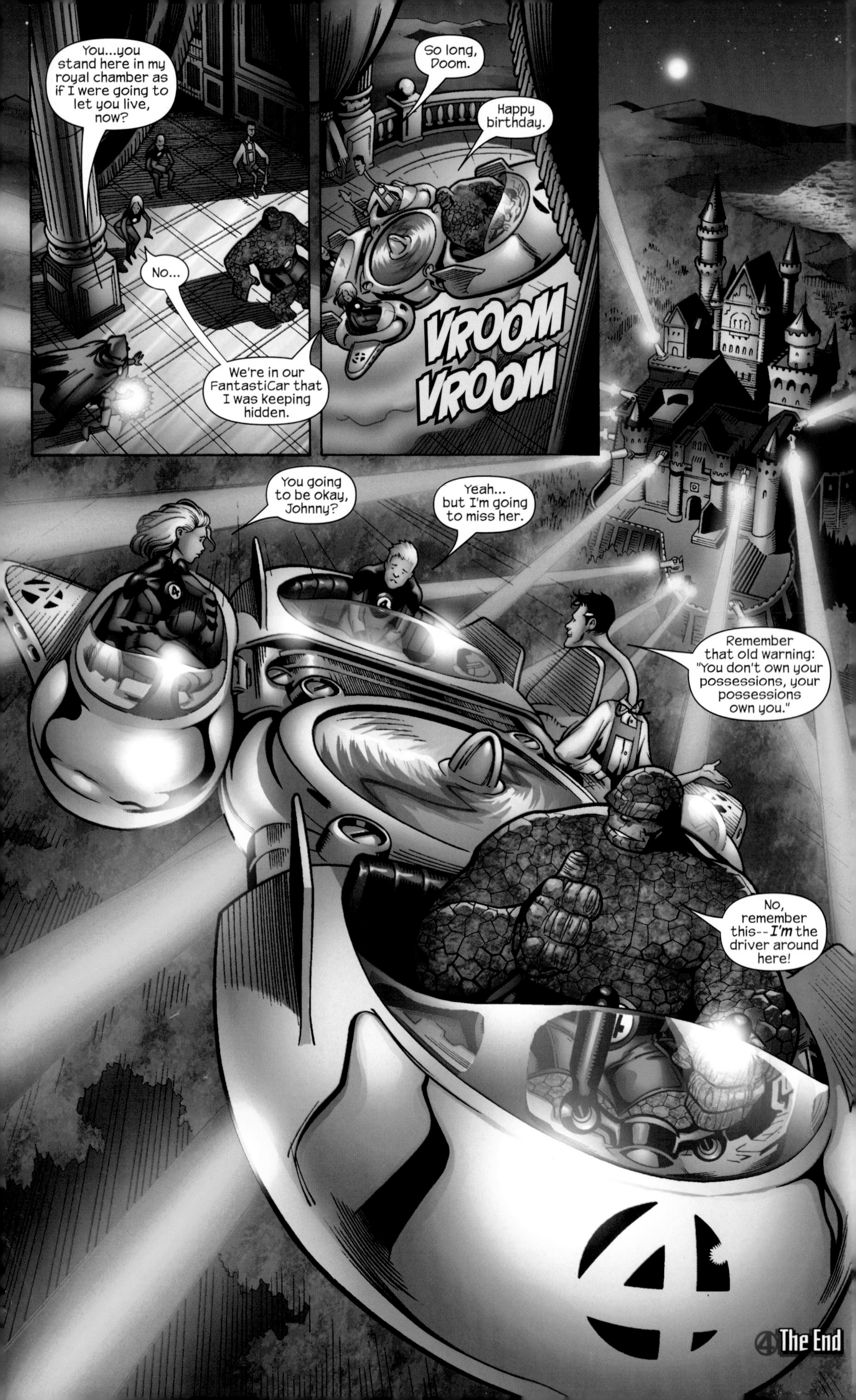
You...you stand here in my royal chamber as if I were going to let you live, now?
No...
We're in our FantastiCar that I was keeping hidden.
So long, Doom.
Happy birthday.
VROOM VROOM
You going to be okay, Johnny?
Yeah... but I'm going to miss her.
Remember that old warning: "You don't own your possessions, your possessions own you."
No, remember this--*I'm* the driver around here!
The End